VOODOO BAYOU

A Shifter Tale of Seduction

****

Maddie James writing as

M.L. JAMESON

I0618293

This is an erotic romance story with paranormal elements and includes a wolf shifter.

Praise for Voodoo Bayou

(formerly titled, *Red: A Seduction Tale*)
This novella takes the everyday werewolf theme and adds a little magic of the Bayou. I was very impressed with how much characterization the author packed into such a short story. Paranormal fans will love the twists and turns into the shapeshifter realm that Maddie takes in this story.

~ Romance Book Scene, Short Story Romance, First Place

Red ... is a sassy, enthralling, and truly a masterful tale of what really went on between Little Red Riding Hood and the Big, Bad Wolf... There was a lot of drama, passion, romance and mystery throughout this book and Ms. James deserves high praise for creating such an incredible tale.

~Amanda Haffery, 5/5 Dark Angel Reviews

She grew up in the bayou under watchful eyes.
Who knew voodoo would bring her back to find her mate?

Voodoo Bayou

A Shifter Tale of Seduction

A modern Red Riding Hood retelling...

The last place Garnet Boudreaux wants to be is back home in Louisiana during Mardi Gras. But with her job on the line, she cannot refuse.

Lured into a voodoo shop on Bourbon Street by her girlfriend co-workers, she realizes the family magic is already at work. Madame Madeleine Dupuis urges her to go to the bayou. The witchy woman presses two pouches into Garnet's hands, wraps a red cape around her, and tells her she must go now—and go now—to see her grandmother.

Max LeBlanc spies the auburn-haired beauty across the street and knows in a heartbeat she is the one. A Rougarou always knows his mate. Some may call him a lycanthrope, a werewolf if you will, but in Cajun bayou lands he's known as *The Rougarou*. He's waited hundreds of agonizing years—for her.

It's time to claim his mate.

Chapter One

Bourbon Street, The French Quarter
 New Orleans, 10:39 p.m.
 "Come closer, Red," he rasped. "I want that burning-hot body next to mine." The wiry stranger threaded hot fingers through her hair at the back of her neck. His steamy breath snaked seductively against the side of her face.

A carnival spun in Garnet Boudreaux's head, and for once, she did not want to get off the ride. Was she drunk? Yes. Was she intoxicated by the exotic passion of the man holding her too intimately for dancing? Oh, yes.

But it was okay, she was with her girlfriends, and they watched out for each other.

Right?

Were they watching his hands glide over her ass, too?

Did she care?

His eyes were dark honey flecked with gold. They pierced hers and held as he pressed closer. His lips scraped over her cheek, sending a shudder of want from her auburn curls to her scarlet toenails. His hips ground into hers as they gyrated to some sort of Zydeco—dancing on a dark dance floor in a bar she hadn't initially wanted to go into.

Until she saw him. Until he crooked his finger and she wandered toward him. Mesmerized, drifting toward him upon demand. Completely under his spell. Her desires out of her control.

Neon swirled as he led her toward the exit door of the *Cat's Meow*, spilling into Bourbon Street's electric currents, taking the lead as they dirty-danced their way into the crowd.

"My friends...," she breathed, wincing as he nipped her neck, his teeth clipping at the tender skin beneath her earlobe. Lightheaded and a bit disoriented, she reached out behind her.

"They're back at the bar," he growled.

Oh damn. She shouldn't leave Tiana and Kathleen behind. They needed her. Didn't they?

Or did she need them?

Like a cat lapping at milk, his tongue laved her neck to cheek. "Give me your tongue," he commanded. His hands rested under her armpits, cradling the sides of her breasts, thumbing her nipples through the red satin dress she'd borrowed for this decadent Mardi Gras party on Bourbon her company had insisted she and her co-workers attend.

Her mask. Had she lost it?

Dammit. She loved that mask. All lace and filigree. It made her look mysteriously sexy.

She glanced behind her, searching through the crowd. He caught her chin between his fingers and forcefully turned her face toward his.

"Me. I'm the one you are with. Forget the others."

Her brain said no. The tingles racing up her spine and the heat gathering in her panties cried yes.

Yes.

His hips teased hers and his dance swept her into a spiral of lights and hands and lips and skin on skin. He dipped his tongue into her cleavage, and she resisted the urge to clasp his head against her chest and keep him there. He was hard against her abdomen.

Ready.

Waiting.

Primal.

Had he growled?

"Garnet!"

A giggle of laughter exploded behind her as Kath, totally lacking in grace, stumbled forward and grasped her forearm. The action spun her away from the man.

"Come back inside! Tiana is giving Jell-O shots off her tits. You have to see this!"

For a moment, Garnet felt disoriented, disengaged, trying to focus on being snatched away from her alluring dance partner and deciphering what Kath was saying.

Tia had Jell-O tits?

Too many Hurricanes. Damn that magic potion of rum and fruit juice, whatever...

A low growl purred in her ear, as if planted there with intent. Calling her. Luring her. Warning her? Turning, she looked back.

He was gone.

At once, she was cold. Empty. Shivering, she wrapped her arms around her chest.

Kath grappled for her hands, tugging her back inside the bar. Garnet tripped backward. Frantic, she scanned the crowd until she saw him. Them. Across the street. A fixed set of brown-gold eyes stared back through the swarm and held for an eternal moment.

Then vanished.

****

"Walk. Now." Garnet grasped Tia by the elbow.

They were on St. Louis Street, around the corner from Bourbon, where Kath and Garnet had dragged Tia from the bar. Red Jell-O stains streaked her chest and the black lace bra that peeked out over her scoop-neck top. She'd just puked into somebody's discarded fried chicken takeout bucket.

"Lost my jacket," Tia wailed, swiping a hand over her mouth.

"You're lucky that's not all you lost."

"Gimmee a break."

"We just did. We broke you loose from that half-vampire, half-Neanderthal creature who was sucking the red stuff off your bra. Gross." Garnet brushed away some slimy goo from Tia's jet-black tresses and grimaced. "It was time to regroup, get sober, and take a walk. Or you were going to be chopped liver somewhere in a dark alley come morning."

"Ne-andre-who?"

"Forget it. Keep walking." They moved through a throng of passersby.

Garnet was irritated and distracted, still looking for a familiar set of eyes with that mysterious element of gold. "I never should have let you two talk me into coming down here again," she mumbled toward the crowd.

They didn't hear her, engrossed in their own little drunken worlds. She'd stopped drinking earlier, after gold-eyes had abandoned her.

Never should have left New York and come back to Louisiana. Damn work convention.

Why did it have to be in New Orleans?

She'd had enough of the poverty and the decadence and the backcountry to last her a lifetime. Years ago, she vowed she would never and now, here she was....

A flash of childhood memories scampered through her head.

Tia jerked her arm and remembrances vanished. "Where we goin'?"

"Back to the hotel."

"Good, I'm gonna puke again."

"Oh, crap." Garnet wasn't the least bit sympathetic. She wanted to go home, where her apartment was clean, the music was civilized, and the crowds—even if they were thick and hurried at times—were not unruly and crude. She wanted a bubble bath and a glass of Chardonnay and Norah Jones on her stereo.

Tired of spoon-raking, accordion-annoying Zydeco already.

Rarely did a man in her Manhattan apartment complex grab his crotch and beckon to her, or a woman lift her shirt to give Garnet a hefty glance at her new boob job.

Yes, she and her mother had done well for themselves after they had left the bayou. She had no desire to return.

Kath tucked Tia between the two of them and linked arms. Garnet figured Kath realized she was a tad ticked. "Hold on, sister, one more block," she said and gave Garnet a *be patient with her* look.

Garnet blew out a breath and moved forward with the trio.

"Ooohhhh..."

"Shit. She's gonna hurl again." Kath's Bronx accent sounded so damn out of place here.

They pushed Tia into the edge of an alley. "Have at it, sister. And be quick. I'm not liking the looks of this wicked place," Kath told her. "Creepy."

Garnet didn't like it either. "Yeah, looks like the kind of place Mr. Neanderthal would hang out. Sure you can't make it to the hotel, Tia? My Jimmy Choos aren't great for running."

Tia answered with a hefty gag.

"Christ," Kath held back Tia's hair.

Garnet kept one eye on the depths of the alley behind them and other on the street. *Good Lord, how could there be anything left in her stomach?*

She glanced into the alley. Something gripped her. Fear?

No. Something else.

Familiarity.

Looking away, she shook off a wet, clammy feeling—like she'd been out too late in the bayou and the mist had settled over her—then dragged her gaze back into the shadowy dregs.

There. That set of eyes. Glistening gold against black.

Watching.

Chapter Two

11:59 p.m.

Tia groaned, flung her black mane out of her face, and then swiped her lips with a wad of tissue she pulled out of her jeans pocket. "God, I hate to sweat."

"You're in New Orleans. Everything sweats here," Garnet countered.

"And right now, you're sweating pure rum," Kath added. "In fact, you reek, girl."

"I do not." Tia stared straight ahead and took one step out of the dark entrance and onto the sidewalk. Garnet didn't argue but agreed with Kath. Rum wafted from her girlfriend's pores.

She followed her from the shadows with Kath on her heels, but not without a backward glance.

Where is he? Gold-eyes?

"Madame Dupuis." Tia said the words matter of fact, like she was waiting for the woman to extend her hand and greet her. "Look." Her gaze was fixed on a shop across the street. Garnet followed the path, a nervous tic plaguing her left eye.

No. Not Madame Dupuis in the flesh, but her voodoo shop.

The building stood on the opposite side of St. Louis Street, northwest of Bourbon. Fewer streetlights lit the area, and suddenly, Garnet wondered why they had ventured this way.

The hotel was in the opposite direction.

"You promised we'd visit a psychic." Tia stared hard at the door front.

Shaking her head, Garnet grasped both women's elbows and pulled them toward the direction of the hotel. "Not tonight. You're drunk. And besides, you need a bath."

Tia wrenched out of her grip and stumbled forward. "Tonight is perfect!" She glanced at her watch. "And it is still early. Barely midnight." She stood straighter. "Besides, I'm better now. Got all that out of my system."

"Nothing left in that stomach, that's for damn sure," Kath grumbled. Then she looked at Garnet. "What the hell? Let's go. I've never been to a psychic."

"Madame Dupuis isn't a psychic."

Tia stretched her arms over her head, exhaled, and pivoted in the middle of the street, looking at the shop. "But it says psychic readings right there on the shop door. Why do you say she isn't a psychic?"

"Because she's not." Garnet dug in her heels. "Come on. We'll find another."

Kath shrugged. "Why? One is as good as another. Besides, this one looks rather authentic."

Madame Dupuis *was* authentic. Garnet knew that for a fact. Madame Dupuis was an authentic witch. "No."

"Gar, come on!" Tia whined.

Garnet swung her gaze back toward the shop. A shiver ran over her. Not dread. Or fear even. It was almost...sexual. Which was oddly misplaced and worrisome.

Without warning, a humid breeze spiraled her hair around her face like a hot breath, raising the hackles on her neck. A low growl rippled in her ear and at once, every one of her senses were heightened, grew more aware. She spun and looked around.

Is he out there?

"Garnet? You okay?"

She nodded, searching the street. "Yes."

"Let's go into the shop. Just look around then," Kath said. "Besides, it's a full moon. Spooky, huh?"

Yeah. Spooky.

Garnet ignored Tia, instead glancing at the sky and the moon. Again, a longing swept over her and propelled her forward. She ran a hand over her head, finger-combing her hair back in place, and then squared herself and looked at the shop.

An awning, once a bright green, hung weathered and dingy over a single door of the French-inspired shop front. The moon cast an uncertain shadow over the door. A sign hung in the window that simply read *Voodoo* in bold red letters, and then another read *Tarot Readings,* and underneath in smaller lettering, *Psychic*. On the door, etched in gold script, also worn by time, the name of the shop's proprietress, Madame Dupuis. A name she knew well.

It was the name that had wreaked havoc and fear, doubt and question, throughout her childhood.

Garnet didn't believe in magic, voodoo, or anything psychic. No. When she left the bayou, she'd put all that behind her. She had no intention of bringing up that hurtful past right now, even to her friends. The peeling letters niggled, however. How long had they been there? Something didn't fit.

Odd that her aunt had moved into the commercial realm of the French Quarter.

Madame Madeleine Dupuis, her grandmother's sister, had always been a backdoor seer of the future. Whether you called her a Voodoo Queen or a swamp witch, the results were all the same. She played voodoo like it was a deck of cards—dealing out the fate of others, poised firmly in her hands—in the backwoods, and occasionally in the back alleys and shadier parts of the city.

Magic.

Spells.

Garnet hated the spells. Things happened when Madeleine Dupuis cast them. And Garnet wanted nothing to do with them, or to be around when they were cast.

But why was her Aunt Madeleine here? In New Orleans?

Times in the backcountry must be hard—*real hard*—for her to leave the life she was born and raised in to open a shop and seek her profits from tourists. She'd always been one to shy away from commercialism of her craft. She preferred her clients to come to her in the bayou, or to meet them in the shadows. That way she knew they were serious about what they wanted, or needed.

Or what they wanted her to do for them.

As Tia grasped her hand, jabbering on like a tipsy little magpie, Garnet wondered if her aunt had always had a presence here in the quarter? If she had, it was not known to the family—or at least, to Garnet and her mother.

Something felt out of place, but she couldn't put her finger on it.

Still, some uncanny pull inched her toward the shop.

Like when gold-eyes had seduced her into their dance, her brain saying no and her body saying yes—this pull to step into the shop was the same. She didn't want to go in, face her aunt, hear her dire predictions, and talk of the turns her life had taken. No. Her life was fine, safe, predictable, and buried in the masses of New York City.

Where no one knew who she was.

Best of all, it was nothing like living in the bayou.

Something buried deep inside her soul propelled her forward like a bumblebee to butterscotch. She was powerless to stop it.

Of course, Tia was also pulling her like a third grader dragging her parent onto a roller coaster ride.

Roller coaster.

If she walked in there, she'd step right into it. A roller coaster ride, much bigger than the dizzying carousel she'd ridden as she danced with gold-eyes, and she feared it would change the path of her life.

Perhaps forever.

Because no matter how much she may want to convince herself that she didn't believe in magic, voodoo, witches, and such, she was fooling herself. Magic was real. Powerful. Witches were real, and not to be taken lightly. Running away from these thing, instead of moving toward them, was her best defense.

If she could.

****

Max LeBlanc shifted his stance, pushing away from the crumbling brick of the shop wall in the alleyway. He slunk forward, keeping close to the wall, his breathing deep and even. He stepped from the shadows and lingered at the edge of the sidewalk, watching Red. His intimate stare played over her as his hands had done earlier in the night. They itched to touch her again.

Clueless. Yes, she was that. But wary.

He could sense her hesitation, smell it on the breeze. Skittish. Fearful of stepping into the shop.

He knew her fear like he knew the back of his hand. Like he knew the curve of her ass.

Whatever she sensed, he felt it as well. Their connection earlier was brief but carved inside him like a stone etching. He sensed what she sensed, felt what she felt.

Her scent wafted toward him and his nostrils flared. It was a unique scent, one he'd not before experienced. She put forward a sweet essence of innocence and sultry spice, peppered with a musk and earthiness that drew him like no other.

He watched as they approached Madame Dupuis' shop, her friends stumbling and Red pulling away at the same time.

Go, Red.

He willed her forward as the trio approached the door. He studied the slink of her skin-tight red dress, the cascade of dark auburn curls water-falling down her back. The length of her firm legs. The rounded contours of her body.

He remembered getting lost in the emerald depth of her eyes.

His breathing deepened, scratchy from his throat. Even. Determined.

A crowd of young people burst through the psychic's shop door as Red's friend reached for the door handle. Drunk. Calling out to each other. Bumping into Red.

She skittered to her right. Away.

A young man stopped. Ogled. Said something to her. Touched her arm.

Red jerked and her voice rose.

Max lurched forward, a growl burrowing up in his throat, a warning bark lying in painful wait.

No.

Stay.

Control.

The three women pushed into the shop. The teenage group guffawed and sauntered off. The young man who had approached Red gave the shop, and her, a backward glance.

Max retreated into the shadows, watching them saunter down the street, the snarl dying in his throat. He would have to mark her.

Soon.

Chapter Three

The shop stood empty—except for assorted voodoo paraphernalia, gris-gris, and shelves of trinkets crowding the small room. No other revelers lurked.

Garnet swept her gaze throughout and determined that Madeleine Dupuis was nowhere to be found, either. Still, a sense of being watched trailed her. She tried to shake off the unwelcome feeling. Although she'd lived with that *watched* feeling most of her young life, she'd escaped it the past few years and it was now unfamiliar.

"Look at all this crap." Kath stepped up to a shelf and pulled off a small bag. Dust puffed up. "I wonder what this is for?"

"Gris-gris," Garnet answered.

Kath glanced up from fingering the object. "Huh?"

"It's a gris-gris bag. It probably has some herbs, stones, hair, essential oils, or such in it. Whatever the gods tell the maker to put in. They are usually custom made for a particular person and reason—protection, luck, love, or other things not so great."

Kath eyed the bag. "How do I know what this one is for?"

Garnet looked at it. "You don't. Not with that one. I'd be careful."

Kath placed it back on the shelf and swiped her hands on the thighs of her pant legs.

"Oh, look! Voodoo dolls." Tia snatched one up and turned toward her friends. "This is Kaitlyn back at the office." She squeezed the doll around the tummy. "I hope she gets a bad stomachache. I hate that bitch."

Garnet snatched the doll from her hands. "Don't."

Tia jerked toward Garnet and shouted. "Give that back. I'm going to buy it."

"You don't need it. Things like this are dangerous in the hands of someone like you."

Tia knit her brow. "Garnet, you are so freaking weird."

"Hear what I say, Tia. *Vous deux*."

"What?"

Garnet put the doll back on the shelf and repeated words from her past. "*Vous deux*. You two, you too. What you sow, you reap. You want to get sick?"

Tia clutched her stomach and groaned. "I think I'm gonna hurl again."

"See? Don't mess with voodoo. We are one with the universe. Each thing affects another. If you wish sickness on Kaitlyn, it will come back to you. Karma."

"You don't believe that crap, do you?" Kath stepped up and studied Garnet's face.

"Besides, she's already been sick."

Garnet looked from Kath to Tia. "Look at her." Tia sat on a chair in the corner, bending over at the waist, hugging her tummy and moaning. "Have respect, Tia. For the doll and the magic."

A black curtain behind Tia swept open and the feminine voice preceded its master. "The woman is right. Voodoo demands respect and is ill-placed in the hands of those who use it for dire purposes. Or in the hands of the ignorant."

Garnet watched as her Aunt Madeleine swept into the room on the wings of a colorful flowing skirt. An indigo scarf bound her long black hair, now graying. She laid a pale hand, freckled with age spots and cragged with wrinkles on Tia's shoulder and paused. Closing her eyes, she said, "Health to the child for she knows not what she does. Heal her of this senseless malady." Tia's face rose to meet the older woman's and then she sat up straighter.

"My pain has left."

"Yes, as did that of your friend far away." Madame Dupuis lowered her head and peered deeper into Tia's eyes. "Do not touch my dolls. You do not know of your power."

Garnet watched Tia's eyes grow round as saucers. "I have power?"

"You do and you do not know how to use it."

Tia blinked. "Goodness."

Then, her aunt shifted her gaze, falling on Garnet and fixing it on her where she stood. "Garnet Boudreaux. You have returned."

"Yes. Only for a visit. I'm leaving in two days. It's work."

Madeleine shook her head. "No. It was forecast."

Kath stepped warily closer and slipped an arm through the crook of Garnet's elbow. "What is going on here?"

Garnet placed a reassuring palm on the back of Kath's hand. "Nothing. It is all right."

Aunt Madeleine interrupted. "It's not all right. Your grandmother needs you."

Stunned, Garnet looked again to the older woman and held her gaze. "I have not seen my grandmother in years."

Madeleine nodded. "Precisely."

"I do not know why she would need me."

"Ah, but she does." The psychic turned away and pointed upward, shaking a finger in the air. "It is because you have not visited her in so long that she needs you." She twisted back and stared, her skirt whirling around her ankles. "She needs you and you must go."

The atmosphere in the room suddenly altered, charged with something akin to electricity.

Static lifted the ends of Garnet's curls and raised the tiny hairs on her forearms. Her friends felt it, too.

"My arms are prickly." Tia shivered.

Kath stood, mouth agape. "Garnet," she interrupted, not taking her gaze off Madame Dupuis, "what the hell is happening?"

Tia inched closer.

"She is my aunt," Garnet told her friends. "Madame Dupuis is my grandmother's sister."

Kath jerked back. "Well, I'll be damned. Your aunt is a psychic?"

Madeleine chuckled.

"That and so much more," Garnet explained. "You don't want to know."

"Enough." Madeleine waved her hand in the air again. "There are tasks at hand. Now, chitchat aside, we must get down to business. Garnet, it is time for you to go. Now."

Her aunt remained insistent.

"I cannot do what needs to be done. I am too old to leave the city and make my way through the backwoods to my sister. You are young and spry and more than able to make the trek. You are to go." She moved behind the counter where an ancient cash register sat. *Cash only*, a small sign read, the tape holding it up yellowed and curled. Evidently her aunt didn't take Visa or American Express or anything close. Bending over, she fished through some items tucked back in the corner of a dingy glass display case.

"Able, yes. Willing, no." Garnet could be unrelenting, as well.

"She is ill and needs your help," the older woman mumbled.

"My grandmother never needed help from anyone. She made that clear when she kicked my mother and me out of her home years ago. She made us leave, Aunt Madeleine, and we had nowhere to go. I'm quite certain she would not want me now."

"Your mother found her way. As did you."

"It was difficult."

"You survived."

"Yes. And so will my grandmother. She is quite capable of taking care of herself. She is too old and too mean to die."

"You are wrong." Finally, with a grunt, she pulled something up from the depths of the display case and tucked it into a red velvet pouch. "Old women say a lot of things they don't mean. Has something to do with hormones, I think."

"Pish."

"Don't pish me, Garnet Boudreaux! Law, I never..."

Her back was to them now, and Madeleine continued to mumble and fiddle with objects on shelves behind the cash register. Garnet listened, trying to discern if her aunt was chanting under her breath.

Oh boy.

She picked up a random vial of this, or a shank of that. Then stopped her muttering and poked them into the pouch.

One. Two.

She gave a couple of items a good sniff and wrinkled her nose.

Three. Four.

She plucked up what looked to be a tooth.

Five.

She stuck out her tongue to lick a stick of what looked like cinnamon. The grimace on her face, though, showed the spice—or whatever—was rather unpleasant. She set it aside.

Five items. An odd number. She *had* chanted.

A spell? But for what purpose?

"There." Turning, she faced the trio of young women, and then snapped her fingers. "One more thing..."

With a flurry of billowing scarves and skirts, she exited the room through the black curtain and before Garnet glanced from one girlfriend to another, her aunt was back. She held another smaller, red flannel pouch and a wrap in her hands.

"Garnet, come here."

Powerless to refuse, she stepped forward, leaving her friends behind. Her aunt flung a hooded red cape over her shoulders, encompassing her body with a warmth she'd not felt in a long time.

Safe.

Secure.

Right.

Shit!

Madeleine Dupuis, her aunt, the Bayou Voodoo Queen, drew near and placed her lips at Garnet's ear. Her aunt held the cape closed in front, pulling her forward, closer to the older woman's soft body. Her scent wafted up and Garnet inhaled a sense of home and longing. The moist heat of her aunt's breath rasped against her neck.

"Take these things," she whispered and placed the small red pouch in Garnet's hands. "Take this one to your grandmother, child. She will know what to do with it."

Garnet pulled back. "But—"

She pressed the larger one tight in Garnet's hands, too, her own hands with paper-thin skin encompassing them. "The velvet one is for you. You'll know what to do."

Panic-stricken, Garnet pulled back. She did not want to carry some voodoo gris-gris with her name on it. "No, not for me. I... I—"

She couldn't refuse.

Madeleine searched her face, peering into Garnet's eyes. She fingered a ringlet of locks, twisting it around her gnarled finger. "You were always such a pretty child and now you are a beautiful woman," she whispered and then sighed. "Ah, but it is a blessing and a curse for this family. A blessing and a curse." She glanced off for a second, then straightened her back and squared Garnet's shoulders toward her. "You know the way, child. You will know what to do. Be safe. Be aware. Things may not always be as they appear. And at times, they may be as they seem. You have to decide."

"But..."

Madeleine silenced her with a soft finger to her lip. "Go. I will take care of your friends and see them safely delivered home. I will explain to them."

"Aunt Madeleine, I—"

"Beware, child, of the...."

"This is silly. I cannot go back to the bayou."

"Rougarou."

Garnet silenced. Her body stilled and she searched her aunt's eyes. "Seriously, no. You are just trying to frighten me."

Her Aunt Madeleine shook her head. "Use your senses. All of them. *All of them, Garnet.* Do not forget what is inside of you. What you were born to do. Now run away. Time is of the essence. And be wary. *The Rougarou* is not a forgiving beast."

A finger of foreboding raced through her and settled deep in her throat. *Rougarou?* No.

She would not be frightened of the childhood wolf tales told by her elders simply to keep her from playing in the swamp late at night. "No, I..."

A cell phone rang. *Some Enchanted Evening* waltzed through the charged atmosphere.

Startled, Garnet reached for her purse. "Mine."

Madeleine nodded. "Answer it."

She did. Her mother's voice, hurried and stressed, broke through from the other end. Shielding the phone away from the rest of them, she turned and whispered into the phone. "Momma, what is it?" Something was wrong.

Garnet listened for a full minute, not once glancing at her friends, taking in every word her mother said. Then, as soon as her breathless mother stopped talking, she snapped the phone shut, paused, and turned back to her aunt.

"I must go."

"Yes," was all Madame Madeleine Dupuis said. "You must go. And go now."

Garnet shared a lingering gaze with each of her friends. "You will see them back to the hotel safely?"

"Yes, yes." Madeleine nodded.

Satisfied, and with a whirl of her cape, Garnet left the shop, setting out on an unwelcome, but necessary journey, carry gris-gris she didn't want to carry, but must.

Garnet Boudreaux was going home. To the bayou.

To save her Grandmère.

Perhaps to save herself.

****

When Max spied the lovely redhead across the street earlier in the evening, he knew in a heartbeat she was the one. He was certain Red had no clue. None.

He had waited a long time. Although impatient, he'd wait longer.

But not forever.

There.

There she is now.

Slinking low and hugging the brick on the opposite side of the street, Max kept a peripheral watch on her as she hurried toward the intersection of Bourbon and St. Louis, away from the chaos. Wrapped in a scarlet cape, she set out alone, her friends left behind. Guarded, she glanced right and left, and then hurried down the brick sidewalk.

As determined as she was uncertain, she sped away. Suspicious. He could tell from her stance, her rigid posture, and the back-and-forth darting of her eyes, that she had set about to do something that she didn't want to do.

He would trail her. Follow.

The moon lit her path. He glanced up. The yellow orb sat full and bursting in the darkened sky. Waiting. Luring. Time was of the essence. He had to move.

Quickly.

Edgy.

Yes. He was on edge.

He could not lose her.

There. Turning a corner.

Follow. Now!

A crowd bustled. Too many people. Where was the red cape?

He thanked the spirit his night vision was keener than his day. There—a flash of crimson. A welcome sight.

He hated crowds. Too many strangers. He preferred packs, or to travel in pairs. In his pack, he knew who he could trust. Not so here.

He needed a mate to travel in a pair. The reason for the moon drawing him away from his pack, out of the woods and into the city, was now clear. Hours earlier, he'd been unaware.

Red.

She was the reason. His. A rougarou always knows when he has encountered his mate—whether by happenstance or fate.

He had waited several hundred years for this moment. To find his mate.

For her.

Red.

****

"Rougarou. Hell."

The word eased off Garnet's tongue and floated into the night as she stepped off the curb and raised her hand to hail a cab. For some odd reason, she couldn't get her aunt's warning off her mind.

Beware, child, of the Rougarou.

Nonsense.

She did not believe those Cajun fairy tales her grandfather used to spin.

"Where I be takin' you, miz?"

The car had pulled to the curb, the passenger side window down. The cabby ducked to look at her, giving Garnet a toothless grin as she positioned herself in the back seat, wrapping her cape around her. By the grace of the gods she'd landed in a cab driven by an older man with a Cajun dialect. She fingered the velvet gris-gris in her palm, the one her aunt said was for her. What did it contain? What was the purpose? Luck? Protection?

"It is a ways. I have money." She'd conjured up her best Cajun dialect, not certain she had pulled it off.

The man's smile broadened. Money would get her everywhere.

"Take me to Acadiana. Bayou country. I'll tell you where."

The cabby let out a whoop and slapped his seat. "All right, miz." He turned and placed his hands on the steering wheel, looking back over his left shoulder to ease into the crowd and traffic.

"I be going home for da night," Garnet heard him mutter under his breath. "*Aissez les bons temps rouler!*"

Let the good times roll, indeed.

****

Max paused as Red grasped the door handle of the yellow cab and slipped inside.

Fear gripped his gut. Unless he hailed another taxi, she would be gone. He swept his gaze about. No cab. She'd be out of sight before he could catch up with her.

The slam of the door startled him, and he darted out from under the dim shadow of an awning.

He raced forward as the taxi moved away from the curb and into slow traffic.

The moon glinted off a tangle of red curls as he loped behind.

Her scent faded.

He watched the back glass. Had she turned to look out?

A snarl moved up into this throat and alarm raced through his chest. He couldn't keep up as the vehicle gained speed. A low growl curled his lips as he moved deeper into the shadows of the street. Running full out now, he shifted—morphed into a creature of the night that could track Red much easier on four legs than two.

He willed the light of the moon to guide him.

Chapter Four

Acadiana, Louisiana bayou, 2:13 a.m.

"We are here, dear, an' I be going to surprise da family now."

Garnet fluttered to consciousness, lifting her head from the back of the seat, and swiping away a line of drool running from the corner of her mouth toward her ear. Her hands still clutched the gris-gris underneath the cape she'd used as a blanket. She sat up straighter and looked at the man. He opened her door and peered in from the passenger side.

The Cajun had chattered her to sleep, the drone of his voice familiar and soothing as she traveled along in the backseat. He spoke of his family back home, not far from where she'd grown up, and was glad he'd be able to visit with them a while this night.

"Of course. I'm sorry I fell asleep."

"No worries, miz. You sleep good, you?"

She nodded. "Yes."

She'd been dreaming, though, lost in a swirl of bald cypress, Spanish moss, and furry creatures in the night. Will-o'-the-wisps, or *feu follet* as the Cajun called them, danced in her head at the marsh's edge while drumming and spinning music made her dizzy.

Grasping the older man's hand, she leaned forward and let him help her out of the cab and back into her cape.

"How much do I owe you?" she asked.

"Near one hundren' and thirty mile. Company man says it should be a lil' over two hundren' an' fifty but I say one-seventy and five dollar."

She gave him all her cash, almost three hundred dollars, appreciating his willingness to cut her a deal. She knew he needed the money more than she did right now. "There. Please have a good time with your family."

Quickly, he counted the money and beamed. "Bless you!"

29

Garnet watched as he rounded the front of the car, then turned back shaking the bills in the air and laughing. "Ma lucky day! *Aissez les bons temps rouler!* Ma family thanks you."

The door slammed and the car engine roared to life. Garnet watched the red taillights disappear on the old dirt road as the hum of the motor faded away. For a moment, nothing but silence surrounded her as she stood alone in the dark. Then at once, the night erupted on the heels of a soulful howl near the edge of the bayou.

An icy tremor ran up her back and she turned to face the sky.

****

Some may call him a lycanthrope, a werewolf, but in Cajun bayou lands he was known as *The Rougarou.* Top Dog, or rather, Top Wolf. He was more than Cajun folklore the locals liked to spin—he was real.

He'd gotten a bad rap over the years, the stories saying he brought death and cast bad spells, but the fact remained that who he was—or what he is—was of little consequence to most people. To live the life he'd lived, part wolf, part man, for nearly three hundred years, was not only a hardship, it was lonely.

Three hundred years was a blip on the screen in the life of a lycanthrope; he was a mere young adult. And, it was high time he found his mate and put an end to his loneliness. He would be a better leader for it.

Restless. Yes. He'd noticed it of late.

His pack had noticed it, too.

They were small and strong in the bayou but waiting for direction from their Alpha.

He'd become the Alpha recently by default, their leader and his mate having succumbed to an illness that struck half the pack. He was the oldest and the strongest of the younger generation, able to fight for and win his position.

But he needed a mate. And none of the females in the pack fit his needs.

A difficult situation, he knew.

Finally, it was coming together. The reason he'd been drawn away from the bayou and into the city. The moon. The calling. The spells.

For a reason.

Red.

And should they mate by the light of the full moon this night, they would be paired forever.

The thing was, there was a little-known fact about rougarous. A rougarou could not know for certain which way he would turn when ritually mated with a human.

He could turn wolf. Or he could turn human. Or he could remain rougarou. For all time.

The answer rests with her. Within whatever molecule etched within her DNA that propelled their fates forward.

The mating was not without risk.

Once consummated, he could be with her forever—or he could lose her for always. For *if* they mate and he turned human, and she turned wolf, their paths would never cross again.

It was genetics. It could even be magic. It may simply come down to the coupling.

Anything was possible.

****

Moon glow bathed her softened features as Red stood looking into the night. Max eyed her slight form, the large cape swallowing her. She appeared vulnerable but stoic as she challenged the night and all it would bring.

For it would bring much. That he knew.

He breathed in and out with slow, methodical breaths. Her scent wafted to him on a breeze, mixed among the odor of the musty decay of the swamp. He could cull out her smell on the head of a pin if he had to. There would be no mistaking this woman from all others for the rest of his days.

The heady scent aroused him, particularly here in the bayou, his home, and begged to rush him closer to his goal. But he knew he must wait. Be patient. Had to restrain himself. The timing was important and he could ill afford to screw up. As much as his body wanted her at this moment, and as much as she was easy prey, he would wait.

His soul wanted her more.

For when he took her, he would take all of her—body, mind, heart, soul, spirit. He would take her willingly, not by force. She would be his, but of her own choice. Seduction was all he needed.

And seduction often took time.

Time was the one thing the past had always granted him. Tonight, however, there were limits. So, the spell of seduction he planned to weave around her would have to fall into place soon.

He prayed to the spirits that if Madame Dupuis had cast a spell upon her, it was one that would contribute to his plan.

He watched her glance to her right, away from the moon and the dirt road where the cab driver retreated—a man whose common sense told him to get out of the woods at this time of night. A common sense Red had dismissed. But something drew her into the bayou, he knew, and the danger of the night played second fiddle to that pull. He watched as her gaze danced along the horizon of the bog, at the edge of the trees, her head cocked to one side.

Listening. Cautious. She took a tentative step forward.

The breeze shifted. She paused, staring ahead.

There, he heard it too.

She moved along a path and into the woods.

He followed, as stealthily as his four legs could carry him.

****

The *feu follet* danced for real this time beside her, not just in her head, as she took the path into the woods. Curls of bald cypress knees pushed up out of the swamp to her left, casting eerie shadows in the moonlight. Faery lights skipped and popped over the marsh near the water's edge. Between the lights and the full moon, her path was well lit.

While she'd grown accustomed to walking the streets of her New York neighborhood in the dark evenings unafraid, traveling the backwoods of the bayou was not much different. Within a few minutes, she was just as comfortable here, as she was back in the city. The environments were different, to be sure, but eerily similar and familiar.

Both felt like home.

She took measured steps forward, fighting an incredible sense of being watched, the same sensation she'd felt in the Quarter, and resisted the urge to glance over her shoulder.

Never look back on a path once taken.

Her grandmother's words rang in her ears, the essence of her maternal elder growing stronger with each step into the woods.

Move forward, always, assured in yourself and your step.

She wondered, if she glanced back into the night, would she see a set of gold eyes following her?

No. Of course not. The mysterious man with honey-gold eyes was far away from this gawd-awful backwoods.

A rustle in the brush startled her and her step quickened.

A soft sloshing at the bog's rim reminded her of the night creatures and she wondered if a gator followed her along the trail, or if a snapper had slipped off a log into the water. No matter.

As long as she kept her head, didn't panic, and moved forward, she would be fine. She grasped the two pouches in her hands and tucked them deep into a pocket inside the cape, which she then pulled snug around her neck.

"I pray for protection," she muttered, hoping one of the pouches was indeed for that purpose.

She knew from the stories she'd been told as a child that the *feu follet* could be the spirits of children who died before baptism, or of other lost souls who had expired in the bayou. Some believed the bobbing lights predicted death. As a young girl, her grandfather would frighten her with those tales, but time and again, she'd refused to let him see her fear.

Outwardly, she showed little fear now. Inside, her guts quivered.

Her grandmother always pooh-poohed the notion of pending evil. She preferred to teach the children that will-o'-the-wisps were magical lights, ones that belonged to faeries and elves and could help guide her home if need be.

Guide her home.

Had Grandmère sent the *feu follet* to light her way?

She had walked this path many times in her youth. It was a mite more overgrown than it had been years ago but was still wide enough to let her through. The visitors to her grandmother's home must be fewer than in previous years. She wondered if that had anything to do with her Aunt Madeleine leaving the bayou, or her grandmother's illness.

The ting-a-ling of a triangle wafted toward her, reminiscent of a musical tinkling she'd heard earlier, and kept rhythm with the graceful ballet of the *feu follet*. The lights twinkling before her down the path remained fixed, not flitting and sparking as they led her forward. Soon a whining violin and the cranking of an accordion joined the ting-a-ling. And she realized as she drew closer to the clearing what she had stumbled onto. A small house—her cousin Renee's—was lit up both inside and out. People milled about and the Cajun two-stepped on the porch and in the yard.

"*Fais do*," she whispered and smiled. She'd not attended one since she was fourteen and Bobby St. Andre had come courting.

As she broke through the path, the faery lights gave way to a cacophony of laughter, singing, and backwoods music and dancing, the likes of which she'd not seen in some time. For a moment, it warmed her heart.

Then she pushed it away.

"Law! If it is not Garnet Boudreaux!"

A myriad of faces rushed forward and welcomed her into the fold, and before she realized it, Garnet was caught up in a two-step with a boy she knew from high school, her cape flaring as he swung her around and dipped her, her feet clumsy at first, but finally tripping in time to the fast-paced Zydeco.

The music stopped and most people wandered to the porch for another beer or something harder. The band fiddled with their instruments as they conversed in the corner of the porch. She wondered if they found it odd that she had shown up here in the middle of the night unannounced.

Absurd, she reminded herself. Family was welcome anytime in the bayou.

Cousin Renee, a man five years her senior, swept her up into a bear hug. "Garnet, I never thought we'd see you again. What brings you here, you?"

"Grandmère. I think she is ill," she blurted, breathless.

She expected to see sadness in his eyes as she said those words, because she felt her grandmother was near death, but instead, they twinkled and sparked something different. "Eh, well, your Grandmère is a feisty one. She'll pull through by the grace of God or voodoo." He cackled then and swung her around. "Let me get you something to eat."

She nodded and he left her alone, standing in front of the porch. The music started again and this time, it was something slow and bluesy, not Cajun. She noticed couples gravitate toward each other as she glanced off to where Renee had gone. He was nowhere to be seen. Then as she looked back, her gaze landed on a man standing at the end of the porch.

A man with sparking gold eyes and desire etched over his face.

Her breath caught in her throat. "How? Why are you here?"

She whispered the words, but knew he couldn't hear her. Still, her brain reeled with trying to reason why this man, whom she'd left behind on Bourbon Street hours earlier, had trailed her.

Or how?

Had he followed her through the woods?

His gaze caught hers and held. She was powerless to move an inch. He began a slow stroll toward her and she ticked off each step. The music matched his sultry swagger.

One. Two.

Another.

As he drew closer, his stealth stroll raised the hairs on her neck. Her shoulders prickled with anticipation. Her breathing grew shallow. He never took his eyes from her as he approached. With a few more steps, he faced her, inches away.

Lifting her chin, she looked deep into the man's eyes. The gold essence of them reflected the moon, like twin yellow orbs for irises.

"Your eyes...are incredible," she whispered.

"Better to see your beautiful face, *ma chèr*." He swept away an errant curl with a fingertip.

Garnet shivered at his slight touch.

Her gaze played over his chiseled face and she inhaled deep, drinking in his scent, experiencing a headiness she'd not felt in a long time.

An uncanny calm swept over her.

She was aware of the music and the others slow dancing around her, but somehow they all fell away and the night belonged only to the two of them.

He lifted his hand to her cheek and traced a lazy forefinger to her jaw, his palm cradling and caressing her neck beneath. Dizzy at his touch, Garnet wondered if the word *swoon* was appropriate for what she was feeling, because all at once, she wanted to melt into him and let him engulf her in his arms.

But she didn't.

Until he reached down, grasped her right hand in his left, and drew her into a dancer's embrace. With his right hand, he undid the frog clasp of her cloak and slipped it from her shoulders, tossing it aside near the porch.

A chill ran through her at the loss of the cape's warmth, her skimpy red dress her only protection against the night's chill.

Until he pressed his body against hers.

Her eyes closed as her breasts crowded his chest. Warmth, liquid and welcome, radiated from him and penetrated her body. Her cheek fit snug in the space between his chin and neck, where a glisten of perspiration glazed his stubble beard. He moved then, a gentle sway of his hips, and she stepped with him, slowly, while his hand trailed down her spine and landed at the small of her back. With gentle pressure, he pushed her hips closer into the cradle of his own.

The act was sensual and mind-bending as her pelvis met with his hard arousal.

Passion zinged through her, as base and primal as any sexual urge could be.

They danced, slow and easy, their bodies and minds melding with the folksy blues of the night. His hands played over her and she let them. His lips grazed her cheek, fell to her neck, and nuzzled beneath the drape of her hair. His fingers tangled in the damp tresses at her nape. And Garnet was lost in a sensation and longing she had pushed away for oh-so-long.

"I want you." His breathless admission thrilled her, his hot pant seared her throat.

"I don't know you," she rasped back.

"Ah, only a matter of time."

Time.

Something she had little of. Cavorting with a strange man wasn't on her agenda this evening.

"C'mon, me sweet. Let us slip away..."

Tempted. Yes.

His teeth raked across her jawbone. Desire spilled through her. Her hips kept rhythm with the slow and easy gyration of his body.

The hand at the small of her back eased to her hip and then smoothed upward with rough movements toward her breast. Lingering. Fondling. Then with his palm flat against her, he slid his hand upward over her chest, to her neck, encircling her column, enticing with his fingertips, as he grasped her chin and lifted her face to his.

Garnet opened her eyes and gazed at the powerfully sexy man who stood before her, his stare pillaging her psyche and the depths of her being.

Without a word, he leaned toward her lips, capturing them in a sweet and tortuous assault of firm flesh, moist heat, and unbridled awareness.

Crack!

Garnet broke away at the sound of the gunshot. She whirled as she saw her cousin Renee cock his shotgun and point it into the air and fire another round. The crowd of family and friends stared and formed a semi-circle around her cousin.

"What?" she cried.

"Just scaring away some mangy wolf-dog," Renee drawled, his gaze fixed behind her.

Garnet turned back. Her potential lover was nowhere to be seen.

Chapter Five

The swamp, 2:47 a.m.

The pirogue was tied to a decrepit little dock at the edge of the bog. The rough-hewn dugout looked rickety, but stable in the water. Garnet felt safe enough, though, having been told by Renee that the boat was sound.

"The swamp flooded over the path between here and your grandmother's house a day or two ago," he told her. "Take the pirogue if you cannot get over the path."

It was not her favorite thing to do, canoeing through the bayou in the wee hours of the morning, dodging sleeping gators and other dangers she'd rather not contemplate. But there was no other choice. The bog ran over the path, and her grandmother's home, much further down, was water locked. Wading through the soggy mess, with snakes and gators alike, was not an especially attractive option. Especially when she was wearing the Jimmy Choo heels she'd paid a small fortune for.

Most importantly, she didn't have a death wish.

She edged closer to the boat. The earth squished underfoot and one of her shoes sunk into the mud.

"Crap."

She bent to brace herself on the boat while attempting to lift the foot buried in the muck. A quick-sand-like suction pulled her in deeper.

"Oh, shit."

Her cape dragged in the sludge and the more she struggled, the more her foot sank deeper into the muck.

"Argh! Forget the stupid shoe, Garnet," she panicked. "Get your damn foot out!"

The words rang out through the bog. Seconds earlier, her ears were filled with night sounds—crickets and other singing insects, a dog yipping somewhere, an owl's hoot.

At once, the marsh was silent.

Garnet rose, her foot still stuck. Wary, she glanced about. The silence sent a warning chill up her back and settled in her throat. An uncanny sensation landed with a thud in the pit of her stomach.

Movement. To her left.

Slow.

Calculated.

At the water's edge.

A log drifting, right?

No. Not unless it was drifting upstream.

Oh, shit.

Gator. He'd lay in wait until she moved again. Maybe. How long could she stay like this?

Certainly not until the mud dried up and her foot eased out of the suction. *Keep me safe, Aunt Madeleine.* That was twice this night she'd uttered up that prayer. *I hope whatever you put in the gris-gris was for my protection.*

In an instant, the world erupted. Garnet felt strong arms wrap around her from behind and toss her into the pirogue. With a swift kick, the boat broke free from the dock and skimmed across the water. What followed was a frenzy of gnashing, rolling, water-churning, and growling at the water's edge. Her screams mingled with the clash. It happened so quickly that Garnet couldn't tell who, or what, was fighting the gator.

At once, the splashing ceased, and the gator took its opponent under. More silence.

She sat there, drifting, waiting.

Whatever the gator had taken under couldn't survive for long. And then what? Would the reptile come after her in the boat?

An explosion ripped through the water and up came gator and victim. Spinning. Fighting.

No.

Not victim. A dog had the gator by the neck.

Not a dog. A wolf!

The wolf's growl rent the night and he fought to the death, his powerful jaws clamped into the jugular of the creature.

Garnet screamed again, repeatedly, as the fight continued, and then abruptly stopped with an unexpected silence. The belly-up gator drifted downstream, slowly sinking, his underbelly reflected in the moonlight. The wolf stepped to the water's edge, panting, exhausted, and looked toward her.

Eyes. Flashing gold.

Your eyes. They are incredible.

Better to see your beautiful face, ma chèr.

She expected the wolf to run, but he didn't. He squared himself and leaped into the water, swimming toward the pirogue. When he arrived and rolled himself up into the canoe with her, he was no longer a wolf. He was a man.

A wolf.

Man.

Rougarou.

Garnet sucked in damp swamp air. "No." Then everything went black.

****

Max stroked damp ringlets out of Red's face as she lay in his lap. The boat meandered through the swamp of its own accord, the moon lighting their way. They kept clear of the shadows, preferring to stay away from the shore. The trees didn't block the moon's glow there, for he wanted it to fully light each and every feature of her beautiful face.

Gently, he caressed her temple. Her skin was soft, pliant, graced with a sheen of dew. He would like to keep her like this for a long while so he could study her, hold her close, lay a gentle kiss on her forehead—but he knew soon she would wake from her blackout. And when that happened, he suspected she would be not so relaxed.

Angry, possibly. More than likely frightened.

Wouldn't any woman by the circumstances? How often did a wolf turn into a man before one's eyes?

She moaned and turned into him. His heart swelled at the thought of embracing her again, holding her in his arms, making love with her for a lifetime.

Destiny would determine that possibility.

Her eyes fluttered, and she gasped upon seeing him, her breath caught in her throat.

****

A dizzy twist of lights and splashing water filled Garnet's mind, soothed by a gentle caress on her forehead. She felt safe. Warm. Protected. A foreign feeling, at best, and it had been some time since she felt this secure.

Where was she?

Her brain limped to awareness. Her eyes batted open; her chest rose and fell with shallow breaths.

Calm. Stay calm.

She woke and looked up. The man with the brown-gold eyes stared down, the pads of his fingers trailing a soft caress over her face.

"Please do not be frightened," he whispered. "I will not hurt you."

Her eyes widened and she realized she was still in the boat, her head cradled in his lap.

"You saved me," she breathed.

Nodding, he agreed, "Yes. And I would do it a thousand times over."

Startled, and remembering the clash with the gator, she sat up and faced him, looking him over. His clothes were ripped. Damp. Streaks of blood ran down his arm.

"You are hurt." She touched his forearm.

He grasped her hand and pulled it into his lap. Her gaze fell there, her hand so small in his large one. "I am... I will be, fine. Do not worry about me."

Garnet remained silent for a moment. *A dream. An unreal dream.* Then she lifted her gaze back his unbelievable eyes.

"Who are you?"

He glanced off into the woods. She studied his profile as he pondered her question, wondering if he would answer. Finally, after swallowing hard, he turned to look at her.

"I am Max LeBlanc."

Garnet shook her head. "No. That may be your name, but you are more."

His gaze lowered and he didn't respond.

"Rougarou," she whispered.

His head snapped up, the gold in his eyes flickered, and a low growl curled his lips. "Yes."

Garnet's breathing quickened and a fissure of something sexual snaked inside her. One moment he was gentle, soothing, the next he appeared ready to lash out.

"I will not hurt you," she repeated his words, wanting him to know she understood. A favorite pastime of the good old boys in the bayou was to hunt wolves, saying they were after the rougarou. She wanted him to know she would keep his secret safe. "Nor will I tell anyone."

"It is you who should be afraid," he countered.

She lifted her chin. "I am not."

"Such a foolish child."

"I'm no child."

But he knew that. With her words, his gaze raked over her as she sat in the boat. Her cape gaped open, half sliding off her shoulders, her short red dress crept up to her hips where she sat. A red shoe graced one foot, the other bare.

Her breathing deepened as she watched him run his gaze over her body.

She slipped the cape off her shoulders and let it drop into the boat behind her.

A low growl radiated from deep in Max's throat.

A warning?

His gaze played over her and with every inch, she felt his touch burn her skin. The slow torture of his perusal drove her crazy with want.

Crazy.

It all was crazy. But for some insane reason, be it the moon or some delicious sexual spell cast upon her this evening, she wanted Max LeBlanc.

She wanted *The Rougarou.*

And if the shallow pant in his chest told her anything, he wanted her, too. She studied his face, his chiseled features, his gray-brown unruly hair, and waited until his eyes—those alluring golden eyes—met and locked with hers.

"Your name," he snarled.

"Garnet." The name feathered off her lips as a whisper.

Their breathing in sync, he moved forward, barely rocking the pirogue from side to side.

She savored the gaze between them.

Inches separated them. She sat on a seat at the far end of the boat, her knees slightly parted, and he kneeled between them, facing her. His gaze trailed downward and landed on her thighs, where he placed both heated palms.

"Garnet."

She sucked in a deep breath and closed her eyes as he touched her, her name tumbling off his tongue. She arched her back and tilted her head to one side. As if choreographed, his lips fell to the crook of her neck... His teeth clamped onto her shoulder. She felt the sting and braced herself. Lower, he began a slow knead of her thighs. Sensation stirred through her, his fingertips stoking a hot flame of desire into her middle, his nip at her neck causing her to jerk in response.

She grasped his shoulders and drew him near.

His mouth played a subtle dance over her shoulder and neck and up to her chin. His scorching breath seared a staccato path to her lips. At once, his hands left her thighs, and he grasped each side of her face as his lips caught hers, a steamy wet kiss offered for the taking.

Garnet had never felt such passion in a kiss. His lips tangled with hers in utter elation.

His tongue slipped between her lips and mingled with hers. His teeth raked and nipped her tender lips and cheeks.

She was lost in a spiral of longing and craving as they mated mouths.

She broke away, breathless. "Your mouth is so...."

"I've only started."

He backed away. His large hands trembled as they trailed down her shoulders, slipping the thin spaghetti straps of her dress down over her upper arms. Heat radiated from his touch, his steamy, breathless pants, and Garnet relished in the feel of it all. She loved the way his touch scintillated. The sensitivity of her skin to his strokes. Then he pulled her dress straps further down and released her breasts from their bondage and into his waiting hands.

With care, he lifted one, then the other, and suckled. He nipped with his teeth and caressed her nipples with his tongue and lips. The sensation shot from the tip of her breasts to the pivotal peak between her legs. Weakened, and having fallen deep into some forgotten abyss, Garnet clasped his head to her breast and held on while he drank his fill of her.

"Max...."

He broke away at the sound of his name on her lips. "Say my name again."

"Max."

He threw back his head and shouted, "Louder."

Breathless, Garnet obeyed. "Max!"

He sucked in a tremendous breath and let out a gut-wrenching howl, his face bathed in the moon. "Yessssss...yes."

When his head lowered to look at her, Garnet caught the flame licking his golden eyes, and realized how primal making love with this man may get.

"Do not be afraid," he whispered.

She shook her head. "N-no."

He waited several seconds, his chest rising and falling with each breath, watching her.

Then he reached for her again, laying his hands on her thighs, his thumbs massaging.

But then he moved lower, sitting back on his haunches, and smoothed the palms of both hands down the length of one leg. Lifting it, he circled her ankle with the fingers of one hand, skimming over a calf with the other. With his teeth, he nipped at the small ankle strap and buckle of her shoe, pulling and tugging until he'd removed it. The shoe slipped off, and he perched her ankle on his shoulder as his hands rubbed their way up her leg, over calf and knee and thigh. His mouth followed suit, licking, biting, and moving toward her center...teasing and tormenting until her thigh was slung over his shoulder and his mouth huffed hot, moist breaths against her panties.

He licked at the outer edge of her panty crotch with the sharp tip of his tongue. He inhaled deep, savoring her scent, and then cradled his face in the juncture of her legs. He paused. Waited. Garnet heard the low growl deep in his throat, rumbling, perhaps restraining.

"It is okay," she whispered.

"I do not want to hurt you," he rasped out. He brushed his chin along her inner thigh. The stubble of his beard only excited her more.

"You won't."

"I'm not certain. I—" He spread her legs apart, and at the most tender and vulnerable spot of her inner thigh, he bit.

Garnet moaned, and found it difficult to remain sitting upright. "Your teeth...they..."

A possessive snarl simmered up in his throat. "Better to eat you with, *ma chèr.*"

In one motion, Max pulled her hips toward him, and Garnet teetered on the edge of the seat. She held onto his shoulders while he lurched forward and, with his teeth, bit into the fabric of her panties and tore them away from her body. On a shaking snarl, he tossed them aside. His thumbs spread her apart, her lips open and waiting. He lunged, like an animal moving in on prey, and raked his rough tongue over her wet sex.

He laved, bit, sucked—*Better to eat you with ma chèr*—moving over her while she tangled her fingers in his hair, holding on while he went down on her like no man before him. He hugged her hips and burrowed his face deeper. Garnet tilted her body, wrapped her legs around his shoulders, pulled and held him closer. His tongue penetrated, in and out, in and out. His lips massaged her sensitive mound. He sucked and toyed with her sensitive clit. She moved with every thrust and parry while he wildly tongue-fucked her, driving her quite literally over the edge.

The boat rocked and they teetered on a delicate, out-of-control balance, while Garnet staggered on the edge of a pleasure-pain outburst of her own.

Her orgasm took her quick and with ferocity.

"Max... *Max!*" She shrieked his name. It winged across the bayou on an explosive exhale.

Her body shuddered, wracked with the pleasure he gave her.

She shivered, trembled, and gasped. Weak, she slumped over and fell into him. He caught her up in his arms and held her. Within seconds, he wrapped her snug in the cape, his large arms encircling her, holding her close, purring to her as she came down from her orgasmic high.

She slept then, blessedly slept in his arms, cradled next to his chest, the woodsy and primal scent of him lingering in her lungs.

Chapter Six

The woods, twelve years earlier...

The trail narrowed and she could see the house far down the path ahead. Her grandmère and her momma were waiting for her to get home from school. Garnet looked down at her new red dress and the funny little hooded sweater her momma bought days before in town. She wasn't sure why momma had bought the red one. She'd always been told redheads shouldn't wear that color.

But it didn't really matter. The sweater was warm and a crisp early winter breeze was blowing through the bayou. She shivered and buttoned the hooded cardigan up to her chin, wishing she'd worn knee socks to keep her legs warm. In science class earlier that afternoon, Mr. Bane had said it was only fifty-nine degrees. She bet it was colder now.

Jimmy Pocketts had punched her across the aisle and asked her if he could wear her new red sweater home. She hated when Jimmy teased her. Grandmère always told her that when a boy teased, it meant he really liked a girl. She hoped that wasn't the case with Jimmy. She didn't like him very much and didn't want him liking her. He was big and older—almost fifteen—and dumb as a stump, or so they said. She didn't like him much because he always smelled of lard and fried fish.

Besides, she didn't like to be teased. Not lately anyway. It reminded her too much of her grandfather. He'd passed two weeks ago and she missed him terribly. Grandmère was often plain mean about it and she and her momma argued a lot lately.

Garnet didn't know why. They were so much alike. She could tell that even though she was only thirteen.

"Garnet needs more than this bayou can give her right now," she heard Grandmère say one afternoon while she and her momma were hanging clothes on the line. Garnet had been sitting on the back porch, pretending to rock in the swing and play with her dolls, but she'd heard every word.

Her mother shook her head. "She's fine. Besides, we have no place to go."

Her grandmother looked at her, a clothespin hanging out of her mouth. "No. Before the time comes, she needs to get out into the world. You have to take her, daughter. It is something you have to do. Just because you have not fully made the commitment yourself—"

Her momma interrupted in protest, "We're fine here. What will be will be. She does not yet need to know..."

Grandmère squared her shoulders. Garnet could still see her face to this very day. It was wrinkled and pale and her eyes looked weak. "Soon, you will have to take her. She'll come back when it is time. Of her own choice and answering her own calling. It is not unlike what the rest of us have to do. She'll make the choices, but until then, you have to give her some life experiences." Grandmère eyed her mother. "Do not let your own past mistakes or pain mar Garnet's destiny."

Garnet still wasn't sure what they had been talking about that day. Nor did she care, then.

Except yesterday, when Grandmère told them it was time to leave—for good. She pushed them away and told her and her momma to start packing and making plans.

Today was her last day of school. She supposed it didn't matter anymore whether Jimmy Pocketts liked her or not. She'd never see him again after they moved to the city.

Momma had a friend in New Orleans, and she said they'd go there. She was scared, she could tell by the look in her momma's eyes. Her lids were heavy and droopy like she'd not slept in days. So, she'd try not to make a fuss...would try to do what her momma said, because this was as hard on her as it was on anyone.

"We're going to N'awlins, sweet pea, and then if we're lucky we'll make it all the way to New York City. I think we can make it big there.

What do you think?" Her mother had asked her last night while sitting on the edge of her bed, brushing her red curls. "Don't be afraid, sweetheart. We'll make it fine and dandy. Fine and dandy..." Her words trailed off into nothingness while she brushed. Garnet let her. The motions through her hair were rhythmic, soothing, and calm.

Probably her mother felt that, too.

"And when we get to New York City, you'll be the prettiest thing they ever seen," she chattered on, almost like she was convincing herself as much as she was Garnet. "Why, with those green eyes of yours and this pretty red hair, New York would never have seen the like."

The boy jumped from out of nowhere and Garnet screamed, dropping her bag. Books and other stuff spilled out on the dirt path. He grabbed her and pushed her hard into a tree alongside the edge. A sharp pain wrenched up her back.

"Jimmy Pocketts! What are you doing?" She screamed and batted at him but his big hands held her upper arms tight against the tree trunk.

"Gonna get me some of this before you leave, girl. You been flaunting that ass of yours around me for too long now." He bent his head and rubbed his lips across her cheek, toward her mouth. She cringed at the spit trail he left on her skin. Her head was pinned between his and the cypress tree. She tried to push at him with all her might.

"No! Get off me, you big bastard!"

Grandpa would not have liked her using that word, but she figured he'd think it was okay in this case.

One hand pushed up under her red sweater, groping. The other reached for her skirt.

She screamed, "Pa!"

In a flurry, the growling animal leaped onto Jimmy's back. With a rabid gnashing of teeth, bone and skin, Jimmy flung himself backward and sideways all at once, trying to strike at the animal. The horrid, garbled sound that came from the wolf's throat was menacing and deliberate.

Garnet stood and screamed. Screamed like a banshee and tried to scare the animal away.

Jimmy Pockets was being eaten alive as he rolled on the ground, fighting with the wolf.

The gunshot blasted into the trees above their heads, ripping through leaves and Spanish moss. A second cock of the gun echoed across the marsh. Garnet stood still and watched her grandmother as she aimed the gun straight at Jimmy Pocketts, and not the wolf.

"You hurt, boy?" Grandmère asked.

The boy looked up the double-barrels. "Naw ma'am." He swiped at his sweaty neck with the back of his hand." Not much. Think ah be going now."

Shaking, he stood and the gun barrel followed him. "You be going, you," Grandmère said, "before I put a load of buckshot in that ass."

He pulled his shirt about him and started to limp away. Garnet noticed that his arm and back were bloody and he was bit all to pieces. But he was a big, dumb kid and he just walked on back home.

"I'll be back an' shoot that damn wolf," he muttered under his breath.

Grandmère cocked the gun and sprayed buckshot into the trees above his head. The boy spun at the crack. "You leave my wolf alone boy, you hear?"

Jimmy Pocketts turned and ran. Garnet never saw him again.

The wolf, however, stood a few yards away. Watching. Staring into her eyes. Garnet shivered with some unknown feeling, but she wasn't afraid and found it darned hard to tear her gaze away from his.

Then the wolf looked toward her grandmother once more, turned, and left.

Garnet wondered if she would ever again in her life see eyes that color of gold.

****

The bayou, present day, 3:33 a.m.

Max cursed and paced. Damn his lack of self-control.

He'd not been prepared to meet up with Garnet face-to-face again. He needed to watch from the sidelines, but the gator had other plans. Plans he had to take care of, and quick. The thought of her being in danger shot through him like a gut-wrenching thunderbolt, and he'd be damned if he would sit back and let her struggle with the animal alone.

No. Never.

He vowed years ago never to leave her alone in the bayou, to protect her. He'd made a choice back there at the dock when the task was finished. He'd stood at the water's edge, watching the gator float away, uneasy of the fact that he'd killed. He looked up into Garnet's frightened and bewildered face and had made a split-second decision.

He could run from her, or toward her.

He'd run from her once before, in the woods, when her *Grandmère* had frightened away the boy. It was necessary then. The timing was not right.

But this time was different. This time he'd run toward her.

Mistake? Maybe. He was unsure.

In his mind, he'd wanted to comfort her. Protect her. Let her know everything was all right. His body and base instincts, however, had other plans. Try as he might, keeping his libido under control with that set of circumstances was damn impossible. Had he been thinking, he would have avoided that scenario like the plague.

When Garnet came to him, he wanted her to be well-informed. He wasn't sure how all of this would play out. And he wouldn't be blamed for seducing her, and changing her life, without telling her the whole truth.

Neither of them were prepared. Red had no clue yet. He certainly could not put her in a position to make an uneducated decision.

No. She had to know what they were up against. How to tell her...? He hadn't figured that out yet, because when they were within inches of each other, their thoughts made tracks straight for sexual pleasures, abandoning any notion of the consequences of their actions.

Damn it.

Now that he'd had a taste of her though, could he back up? Retreat? Gain control?

He had to. *Had* to.

Time to think. Get this right. They may only have one chance. The hours were dwindling.

Last thing he wanted to do was blow it.

****

Curled into her cape, resting on the bottom of the pirogue, Garnet felt warm, sated, and somewhat fatigued. But she woke with a start as the drifting boat slammed into solid, unyielding earth. Her eyes flew open and she looked up. The moon overhead stood mocking in the night sky, slanting down between two trees. It slipped toward the horizon, telling her she'd slept.

Sitting up, she glanced about. Alone.

Max was gone.

She clutched the cape tighter around her, a sudden chill pushing over the marsh and settling in her bones.

Had he been here with her? Or was the entire episode some sort of delusion.

Dream.

Jimmy Pocketts burst into her head. She'd not had that dream in a long time. It *was* a dream, wasn't it? At the moment, she wasn't so sure about anything.

Sitting up, she glanced around. She was grounded, stuck in the mud. Down the path she could see twinkling lights. Grandmère? Will-o'-the-wisps?

Or were they one and the same?

She didn't know anything anymore, except that she had a quest to fulfill. Reaching deep into the pocket of her cape, she fumbled for the gris-gris. There. Two of them. Still with her.

A sigh escaped her lips. At least that was something.

Standing, she stepped over the seat in the pirogue and bent to pick up an oar. She pushed it into the soft earth at the edge of the water to steady herself as she leaped over the side of the boat and onto dry land. Maneuvering out of the boat was a helluva lot easier with bare feet.

Glancing back, she spied the lone red heel lying in the hull. A vision flashed before her eyes—Max clutching her panties in his teeth and ripping them from her body.

A thrill raced up through her, almost as potent as the moment it had all happened.

"Stop it," she whispered.

Where was he? Why had he left her? Where do men who turn into wolves go when they turn back into a man? Where do they live when they are wolves?

How do they exist?

How do they love?

Tomorrow. I'll think about it tomorrow. I have things to do tonight.

Grandmère's words echoed in her head, crowding out her own thoughts. *"Soon you will have to take her. She'll come back when it is time. Of her own choice and answering her own calling. It is not unlike what the rest of us have to do."*

Was this her time? Her calling?

She stared down the path. The lights danced in the distance. Her destiny lay in wait. She knew that for a fact. Nothing else to do but move forward.

Chapter Seven

To Grandmère's house, 3:43 a.m.

The end of the path was near, and even in the dark Garnet knew she was very close to her grandmother's home. The *feu follet* sprinted in front of her, compelling her forward. At times, it seemed the twinkling lights would bob and curtsey toward her, as if to crook their little imaginary fingers and say, "Hurry, come faster now."

She rushed along at the imagined urging.

Memories trickled back of her time there as a small child. She used to play in front of the shack, the shadow of the rickety porch over her shoulder as she sat and scratched in the dirt with a stick, keeping count of how many jacks she could pick up, or ticking off the number of fireflies she'd caught in a jar the night before.

Hers was a carefree childhood, running barefoot through the woods, wading in the creek, rolling with the puppies in the front yard. Dogs. There were always dogs. Pa had hounds for hunting and momma always liked her mutts, as she used to call them.

Those days were long gone now, and for the first time in almost a dozen years, she was heading back. A strange but welcome feeling crept over her. She thought perhaps she should be frightened. Strange that she wasn't. The closer she walked toward her childhood home, the calmer she felt.

She worried about Grandmère, however, and the condition she would find her in.

Estimating the time of night by the position of the moon, Garnet figured it was somewhere close to four a.m.—not early enough in the morning for the sun to rise, but late enough that the moon slipped low in the sky. It rested round and large over the trees behind the house. A soft glow bathed the area where she knew the house would be.

Her steps were purposeful, pushing herself toward her destination. But at once, she stopped. Stood still. And listened.

A soft hum greeted her, like a swarm of bees in the distance. Chanting.

Layered on top was the willowy soft voice of song. A familiar voice. All of it lured her forward, growing louder with each step as she broke through the clearing.

Her eyes widened at the sight before her.

A fire burned in the dirt yard in front of her grandmother's home. A garland of women circled the flame, their faces lit with fiery flickers against the night. Their voices united in a low chant—even, rhythmic, and precise. Their hands joined as they continued their invocation and looked into the flames.

One voice sang a soft, sultry, siren song. The tone, her mother's, was one Garnet knew well, having listened to it almost every day of her life. The subtle drone soothed her, lured her into the fold, and told her all was well. The woman greeted her with warm, welcome eyes.

Garnet broke into the circle, clasped her mother's hand, and studied her face. Her mother returned a gentle smile, nodded, and resumed her song. Garnet felt safe but confused as she glanced about.

To her left, another hand slipped into hers. Garnet glanced that way. Her Aunt Madeleine's thin lips drew up at the corners. A quick grip of her hand welcomed her. Madame Dupuis never missed a beat of the chant she led.

The staccato of their words deepened. She was drawn into the swirl of the spell. Her gaze spanned the ring of women who surrounded the flame, their faces flashing before her. Some family. Some neighbors. Some childhood girlfriends all grown up.

Garnet was taken in, part of the circle, accepted, and mesmerized into the loop. Her breathing deepened and lifted her chest with the rhythm of their recitation.

It all seemed natural, but a fissure of fear—perhaps alarm of the unknown—gripped her and held. Obviously, there were things she did not know. Things she must learn. And her family and her friends were a part of it.

Why had they kept this from her for all these years? For what reason was she sent here this night?

The question burned in her gut.

The flames shot higher and heat bore into her, licked within her. Perspiration beaded on her forehead, ran down her neck and settled in the cleavage of her breasts. The cape was hot and she wanted to toss it. But no, she needed it with her, needed what was in the pocket. Somewhat disoriented, she attempted to swipe her brow, but couldn't pull her hand out of her mother's grasp.

A burning deep in her womb pulsed as the chanting grew louder and encompassed her.

Her loins ached with want...with desire and carnal decadence. She shivered and shook off the feeling. It crept back with wild and wanton abandon.

The faces of the women coiled around her, sometimes human, sometimes not.

Sometimes...wolf? All feminine. It should seem odd, but didn't. Her mother's and aunt's hands gripped tighter. She was caught in a dizzy, drunken swirl of flame and face, song and snarl.

Garnet was unsure whether she could stand on her own or if they were holding her up. She was lost within everything happening around her, within her.

The chant welled from her soul and her lips moved, speaking words she didn't know she understood or could articulate. Singing a song on a whisper she didn't know the lyrics to. Words.

There were none for the longest time, as the chant melded into sounds and guttural utterances, melody and rhythm, yaps and howls of the feminine pack.

Primal. Basal. Ancient.

Grandmère spoke from somewhere in the distance. Perhaps in her mind.

You have a calling, Garnet. You must choose. It is time for a mate. You do have a choice, and this is what you must know: You can walk away, and your life will remain as is. Or you can explore the possibilities and have so much more.

There is a risk.

You may win. You may lose.

But if you do not try, you will never know. And then what?

Garnet broke the ring and turned to her mother. "Stop. Stop!" She clamped her hands over her ears. "Please stop this. I need answers!" For a moment, everything did stop. No chanting, no singing. No growls. There was silence.

"Sweet pea, ask your questions." Her mother brushed a curl away from her sweaty forehead.

"Why are we here? You?"

The expression on her mother's face wavered. "Garnet, I've let some of my past influence your future. It was time for me to make amends. Because I lost my own mate when I was a very young woman, I've been hesitant to let you grow up and seek your own. I was trying to spare you similar pain."

"Momma, what is happening?"

"The young always return to the den, my sweet. It was time. Your time."

"You are talking in circles." She turned toward the others. "Why are they here? What do they know?"

"Time, *chèr*. All will be answered in time."

She was tired of waiting for answers and backed away. "Where is my Grandmère?" she demanded.

"Her spirit is here, child," her mother calmly returned, "but she is no more. She passed yesterday."

Panic raced into her chest. "Yesterday?"

Her mother nodded. "It is why you were summoned."

Garnet shook her head. The chanting resumed in the background. "Summoned?"

"You are requested to take her place, child. You are young and a mate is waiting. But the choice is yours."

"I... I don't understand."

"You will."

A low growl rumbled around them and the chanting deepened, quickened. Garnet turned to her aunt. "You said... You said you could not come. That I was to bring these things to her."

Her aunt nodded. "Yes. That was your task."

"But you are here. Why did you not bring them?"

"It was your quest, Garnet, not mine."

She studied her. "Oh, I see. It was all a ploy to get me here, right?"

"You were lured, yes."

"Lured? You made it quite clear in your shop that Grandmère needed me, that I was to bring these things to *her*."

Madeleine chuckled. "The shop was an illusion, child. I have been here all along. I have never left the bayou. Ever."

Stunned, Garnet let that knowledge sink in. "But the shop...."

Her aunt cupped her cheek. "In your head, sweet. We needed you here. Your grandmother needed you."

"But she has passed! Why did I do this?" She reached into the pocket of the cape and pulled out the two red bags, one velvet, one flannel. "What are these gris-gris all about? Why did I need to bring them if she was gone?"

Madeleine clasped her hands and looked deep into Garnet's eyes. "Your task is unfinished. You will see, soon, that you are a child of the bayou. Take the gris-gris into the house, Garnet. Your grandmother lays in wait. Sprinkle the contents of the small one on her body, say your prayer to her, and then you will know what to do."

Garnet stood and looked deep into her aunt's eyes, then swept her gaze around the circle of women. Held rapt by the chant, the fire, the song.... They clasped hands and stared into the fire.

Their faces distorted. Half human, half wolf.

Half human. Half wolf.

Her mother squeezed her hand and she looked to her. She was the same, except now her brown eyes flickered with a gold flame.

Garnet dropped her mother's hand and moved toward the house, her steps slow and unwavering. The women stayed at the fire. The chants rose behind her as she felt the heat of the flame at her back. There was no song now, nothing to lure her into their fold, the pack of women she now thought of as sisters. She wasn't sure why, she just knew. And with each step forward, with each utterance that moved her onward, and each growl and bark that penetrated her psyche, she realized her destiny was to be more than simply one of them. Somehow, they were looking up to her.

She was to lead them. Guide them. Teach them.

She lifted one foot to the wooden step of the porch. Then another. Her gaze was focused on the entrance. The front screen door stood ajar, the inside door slightly cocked. A cleft of light beyond enticed her onto the porch. She reached for the wooden handle and stepped inside.

"Grandmère?"

No response.

Garnet pushed the door aside and entered the candle-lit room. It appeared the flames followed her inside. The heavy door closed firm behind her and she heard the soft, distinctive click of a latch. Outside, the fire and her sisters waited. The crescendo of their ceremony resumed, comforting her.

In the center of the candle-lit room, her grandmother's body lay on a table. Garnet slowly approached. The rim of flames danced, circling her body. Garnet drew her cape closer around her body, suddenly chilled against a slight breeze coming from somewhere in the house.

Grandmère was dressed in a white gown, her hands folded across her abdomen, her eyes closed as if in restful slumber.

Garnet moved to her, looked contemplatively at her face, and touched one of her soft fingers. Her eyes stung and a tear spilled over and splashed onto her grandmother's hand. Garnet moved her thumb over it and rubbed the salty droplet into the paper-thin skin over her grandmother's knuckle. Although disappointed and hurt by the woman who lay in death before her, her heart ached with the thought of losing her forever. She wondered if her anger was sorely misplaced.

"Forgive me, Grandmère," she whispered. "And help me."

Her grandmother's body lay still, unmoving, without response.

The gris-gris.

She searched for the flannel bag in her pocket and spilled its contents into her palms. A shank of hair, a packet of gold powder or spice, a wax packet of something unknown, a vile of liquid, and several canine teeth. She studied the items and tried to figure out what they might mean. But that was of little consequence now. She'd been instructed what to do with the items in the bag, so it was what she would do.

Her eyes closed, she clutched the items to her chest and said a silent prayer to her Grandmère, wishing her Godspeed and grace as her spirit lifted into another world.

Say hi to Pa for me.

Opening her eyes, she looked again at the collection of items from the bag. The shank of hair was first. She unbundled it and let it lay in her hands. Short and coarse, its texture felt familiar, and as it warmed in her palm, her thoughts flew again to her grandfather. Was this some of his hair? Avoiding the flaming candles, she sprinkled it around and over her grandmother's body.

Where it touched her skin, it clung and held fast. The gold power was next, and as she sprinkled it, the tiny particles flew straight to her grandmother's eyes and settled over her eyelids. Garnet's heart raced as she fumbled with the small wax packet. Slivers of human fingernails broke from the bag and collected into hard points on her grandmother's fingertips. Her chest heaving, Garnet gathered the teeth up in her hands, held them over her grandmother's body, and let them fall. The older woman's mouth opened and each canine fell into place in her jaw. Frantic, Garnet knew she had one last task, and she fiddled with the rubber stopper on the brownish-red liquid in the vile.

The glass burst in her hands. The shards cut her palms. A thick oozing liquid ran through her fingers and dripped onto the floor. Her blood mixed with that from the vile.

"No!"

Knocking candles aside, Garnet moved swiftly over her grandmother's body and let the blood spill over onto her white gown, trickle on her arms, her chest, her face....

A flame rose behind her. A candle ignited a small rug. Another erupted to her right. Then to her left. The drapes....

The room was soon engulfed. A bonfire. A pyre of death.

Or perhaps life?

A flash swept through the room. Out of the fire and off the table, a she-wolf leapt from her grandmother's body, snarled, heaved in one choking breath after another, and stared at Garnet through the growing flames.

"Grandmère!" Garnet screamed.

You've set me free, my Granddaughter. The world is yours. And I will now join your grandfather.

The wolf jumped from the table. The house was engulfed.

"No! I don't know what to do!"

You will.

Chants and snarls surrounded her. The flames fell away. The house was gone. Her sisters stopped chanting.

And she turned.

The fire was no more and the garland of women who once circled the flame were now wolves running on all fours, circling an Alpha and his mate in the center of the pack. The vision before her coiled and swelled with the couple as they morphed into two people she'd loved and cared for all her life—her grandparents. Then, at once, their ghostly images shifted back into their wolf bodies and ran off together into the night.

For a moment, the circle was empty, and the pack stopped their sprint. Aimless, they glanced about. Searching.

A howl rose from the bayou and Garnet felt every decibel of the sound resonate deep inside her bones. The call was for her. Her skin prickled with sensual longing, as if his fingers trailed over every sensitive nerve ending she possessed. Her womb heated with warmth and awareness, anticipation, and an intense desire for fulfillment.

Max stepped from the woods and moved to the center of the pack. The wolves looked at him and gradually began their spiral trot. All the while, his golden eyes never left Garnet's.

Breathless, she faced him and knew from this moment on, her life would change forever.

Had she possessed the answers all along?

Lead them. Guide them. Teach them.

To do that, she had to have a mate.

****

His chest about to burst, Max stood looking at the most beautiful woman in the world.

His woman. His mate.

If she would have him.

He didn't know yet what she knew or expected. All he could do was stand and stare as he watched her chest heave with each breath she took, and her gaze entangled with his.

The memory of their all-too-brief encounter earlier in the night plagued him. He yearned for more. Wanted, needed more. The taste of her was still ripe on his tongue. The feel of her tender skin scalded his hands. Her scent riddled his nostrils.

He craved, required, hungered for more.

Those brief encounters would never be enough.

He feared she would not step into the circle. And he prayed she would.

If she moved forward, joined him in the circle, there would be no turning back. The ritual mating had to take place this night, beneath the full moon.

He glanced at the pack, circling him madly. The moon fringed the trees above them. A hint of red streaked the sky at the horizon.

The night was leaving.

He could not wait another cycle to have her. He'd go mad with need should she falter.

Apprehension ate at him... Should they mate, and he turn human, and she wolf... Would they be lost to each other for eternity?

He would endure. She was his. And he meant to have her.

Only the fates knew. It was rare such a thing should happen. In the history of rougarous there was a story of just one mating gone awry... One coupling that ended in tragedy... One Alpha who was rejected and lost his mate for life. His death at the jaws of his pack was a pitiful and sad way for an Alpha to die.

Though all signs pointed to the fact that she was the one—that she was the sole human who met his needs for a match—he feared something amiss.

Her faith, however, could be the key. Did she believe? Could she commit?

Submit?

Patience....

No.

This night did not call for patience. It called for something more primitive and lustful.

Seduction.

Chapter Eight

Though the fire had now dissipated, a cloak of heat still radiated about her. Garnet felt every scorched breath deep inside her lungs. She panted—her chest heaving in and out in rapid thrusts—as she stood on the ring's perimeter of rapidly moving animal flesh. Paws pounded the earth, jaws opened, teeth reflected the moon, and saliva dripped trails behind them.

Orbs of gold flashed as they made eye contact with hers.

She followed the coil as it wove around Max and, at last, lifted her gaze to meet his. They locked, held, and Garnet felt a current rush through her like none she'd ever felt.

Propelled forward, she took one slow step, and then another. The wolves surrounding Max widened the circle and as she moved toward him, the dance of their paws excited her and made her feel dizzy. Soon, she found herself inside the fold.

Her brain reeled and as she stood, looking at Max, their gazes still connected, she ran through a litany of dialogue, trying to make sense of what was expected of her...of what her next move should be.

"Come closer, *ma chèr*," he whispered. His hot breath snaked out and scorched her lips, even though several feet still separated them.

I am to make a choice.

I am to lead. Guide. Teach.

I am to choose a mate.

I am to believe.

Of these things she was certain. Of other things, she was not.

Would it be enough?

Max stood solidly in the center of the ring.

"I... I am not sure what to do," she whispered.

"Come to me. I will not hurt you. I have not hurt you."

He had not. She trusted him earlier in the pirogue. He saved her from the gator. Earlier in her life, he had saved her from Jimmy Pocketts. He was her protector. Was he also her mate?

"I do not know what will happen." In all the world, what she wanted at that moment was to collapse into his arms, come into him and become one with him—to feel safe and secure and wanted.

"Have faith, Garnet. What do you want to happen?" He stepped closer.

She knew what she wanted. She wanted Max, and she wanted him for all time. But he was a wolf. A man. A rougarou. What did that mean for her? How could she love a man who was half-wolf, half-human?

A vision of her grandparents flashed before her. Was it true? Were they rougarou?

Was she?

Was that her life path?

"Things change, my love, in our lives. Sometimes for the better." Max took another step. "I will care for you always. Love you. See to your needs. Provide for you. Make love to you each and every night like no other."

Garnet found herself countering his stride and timidly moved closer. First one step. Then another. Quicker. Until breathless, she stood before him.

He dragged a forefinger down the side of her face. Garnet's eyes closed at his touch, shivering as the tingle ran the length of her body and settled in her belly. Her heart beat in rapid anticipation of more. More of his touch. More of *him*. "What will happen?" she whispered.

The pack yipped, yowled, and snarled with each other. Almost rabid and frenetic, as though incited by something... Some tension that held them on the verge. She opened her eyes and looked at them.

Max snatched her chin in his fingers and pulled her back to look at him. "The night is leaving. The pack needs to move to their dens. And I need to tell you one thing."

Garnet searched his face. "What?"

"You are mine, Garnet. Mine. My mate. My chosen. I want you."

"I want you," she whimpered.

"Do you know what that means?"

"No."

"It means you are making a conscious choice. If we mate, tonight, here under the moon, things will change. We do not know how. But the key may rest with you."

"Tell me."

"You may become like me, a rougarou, for the rest of your life. Half-human, half-wolf. And I will stay as I am. We will be the same."

"But something could go wrong?"

"Yes."

"I want to know."

Before he answered, he grasped the back of her neck and pulled her forward. A sensual thrill welled inside her as he dragged her closer. His lips claimed hers in an all-consuming, powerful kiss.

He broke free. His chest rose and fell with a powerful exhale. "I could turn wolf. Forever."

He paused. Garnet added, "And I could stay human."

"Yes. Or vice versa."

Garnet took in all he said.

It is a risk.

You must make a choice.

Garnet slipped her hand in the pocket of her cape and placed it on the velvet pouch. The answer did rest with her. Aunt Madeleine would not steer her wrong, would she? With her hand fingering the soft velvet, she looked into Max's eyes.

"I choose you," she said. "Now."

****

On a whirlwind of chant and song, of barks and bays, and of dancing *feu follet*, Max swept Garnet into his arms and transported her deeper into the bayou. She clung to him as they speedily moved through the night—not fully comprehending how they were moving so fast—her head buried in his chest, his arms wrapped securely around her.

They landed with a soft thud on a bed of moss and leaves, tucked beneath an umbrella of cypress and veiled in Spanish moss. The dark cave made by the foliage was penetrated only by the soft yellow glow of the moon, perfectly framed by branches above.

Garnet looked at Max. "I am not afraid..." Her voice was soft, hushed.

He took her face into his hands, cradled it as if she were a precious jewel. "I love you,

Garnet Boudreaux. Red." His kiss was soft, seductive, spellbinding.

"I love you," she breathed against his lips. Closing her eyes, she took his woodsy scent deep into her lungs. "Whatever happens," she whispered, "know I will love you always."

"And I you..."

His mouth raked across hers, hot and moist, searing the tender skin at the corners of her mouth. He bit and tugged her lip, sending a frisson of want through her body, and urged her to the ground. With deft fingers, he undid the clasp at her throat which held the cape together and spread the red fabric on the ground.

"Wait," she said, sat up and slipped her hand into the pocket. "There is something I must do."

She removed the pouch and released the drawstring. Max watched as she emptied the contents. Two items tumbled onto the lining of the cape.

"My aunt sent this with me, said it was for me. I thought perhaps it was for protection. Now, I am hoping it is for more...for us."

Garnet first lifted the vial of liquid, removed its stopper, and sprinkled it over the cape. A musky scent greeted them, as the essential oil anointed the fabric. A soft mist rose from the oil and she tugged Max closer. She then followed the liquid with the small baggie of powder, sprinkling it liberally into the mist. The fog rose and shrouded them with a heady fragrance.

Garnet took Max's hand and pulled him to her as she lay on the cape. His body covered hers and the primordial dance began.

She reached for him and framed his face with her hands. Their lips crushed in a meeting of longing and ache. Garnet struggled for breath, hers leaving on hurried exhales and panted gasps as Max's kiss took her under. He matched her rhythm of breathing with his own.

His hand slid to her thigh, lifting the hem of her dress. Her panties long gone, he sought her center. His fingers teased, taunted, and played over her mound. She opened to him as he probed inside her tender flesh. Faint with the essence of the night, or perhaps it was some spell cast on them from the gris-gris, Garnet inhaled the mist and was lost in sensation and yearning.

As his palms skimmed over her hips, the red satin dress bunched around her waist, and Max straddled her body. Grasping the thin straps, he lowered them, smoothing his hands over her shoulders. Garnet felt warm and safe... Wanted his hands on her... Waited for his mouth on her breasts, for she knew where he was heading. He released each one of them then, pushing her dress down around her waist. The red satin became a band around her middle, her upper and lower body fully exposed.

To Max. Her lover.

Soon, her mate.

He suckled and she moaned, the points of her nipples drawn deep into his mouth. Garnet could feel the sensitive tug, jolting her into a deeper state of arousal. She moaned his name as his hands palmed her breasts. In tandem, he purred, a low and steady growl from his throat. His hips gyrated against her pelvis, starting a lazy and deliberate pumping against her, his erection firm and powerful against her belly.

He stroked himself against her pubic bone and her instinct drove her to spread her legs wide in preparation to take him in.

He left her breast and moved his hot mouth higher, to her neck, her face, shoulders, scraping his lips over her damp skin and leaving a trail of heat behind. The tremor deepened in his throat and Garnet found the resonance sent a sexual spiral through her like a mating call. His mouth clamped over her shoulder, and before she realized what was happening, Max sank his teeth into her. With a slight puncture of the skin, the point of his entrance was both startling and sensual.

"Max..." she moaned.

"I will not hurt you...please, *chèr*...trust me."

****

Max felt the growl rumble deep in his throat. He marked her. A small nip on her shoulder, his teeth imprinted on her skin. He lapped at the small amount of blood, licking it clean, the metallic taste of it untamed on his tongue. His lips ripped down her body while he surged lower and settled his face in the crook of her thighs.

Pace yourself, he warned.

"Trust...you..." Garnet hissed. He knew from the rasp of her voice that she was lost in their lovemaking.

His.

His mate.

Her scent penetrated deep into his nostrils, and it was all he could do to contain himself.

He didn't want to restrain, and yet, he did. So fearful of hurting her...so aware of the primal and delicate dance in which they were partaking.

With his thumbs he spread her lips wide and opened her petals. With one long lick, he swiped the flat surface of his tongue over her, from bottom to top, and then lingered and teased her hot and protruding nodule.

She shouted and clutched at his shoulders, his head, and Max closed his eyes in the sheer bliss of it all. Before long, no amount of restraint would hold him back. No amount of manly control was going to tame the beast about to burst forth in him. For whatever kind of beast he was, at no point in his life prior to this, had he felt the urge to mate, dominate, and procreate as strongly.

A powerful eruption, a hundred years of unfulfilled longing, welled inside him and at once, Max reared back on his haunches and looked at the moon. The howl that escaped him was not that of a man, but of a wolf.

He looked to Garnet through a golden haze, and watched her moan in unsatisfied sexual release before him. He grasped her legs and pulled her forward, turning her over in the process.

His hand skimmed over her sweet ass and then he urged her onto all fours. He grasped her hip bones and pulled her backward. He wanted her. Needed her now. Wanted to plunge himself into her.

But not before he tasted her once more.

Reaching between her legs, he cupped her, and then slid his middle finger deep inside her. Garnet threw back her head, arched her back, and he stretched to grasp a handful of those red tendrils flung over her back. Pulling her hair taut, fingering her pussy, milking her juices, and readying her for him.

Max felt the change coming over him, consuming him, her moans and primal utterances riveting him into the beast he was, would always be. Powerless. He was powerless to halt the transformation. His body thrummed with need, with a primordial urge to capture, tame, possess, own...

She exhaled and sighed with tiny pants of pleasure. He plunged deeper, faster, playing her like an instrument. She hummed and purred, shuddered and moaned. Her legs trembled and her body tensed. And right before she went weak, unable to hold herself up any longer, Max dropped to his knees, spread her apart from behind, and with his long tongue, licked.

It took one languorous lap of his tongue before Garnet exploded in orgasmic pleasure.

Her back arched and she bayed into the night, screaming Max's name from her throat. He grasped her hips and held her tight as her convulsions eased, then he pushed himself into her with a thrust of pleasure that bordered on pain, as she sheathed him in velvet.

His claws scratched down her back. Max plunged his hardened length deep into her, over and over again, locked in a fast and furious propulsion of lust and need.

Her slickness drove him on. The beast in him unleashed as his territorial instincts drove him to claim her, and protect her.

Mark her.

His.

And with one final thrust...one determined and mind-bending compulsion of desire, he drove into her. Poured his seed into her womb, and made her his mate for all time.

His world spun out of control, his brain reeling, his body humming with spent pleasure.

He fell onto her, curled her against his chest and cradled her from behind, wrapped in the red cape.

Chapter Nine

A thin beam of sunshine slanted across the marsh, cut through a web of lacey moss, and taunted warmth across Garnet's cheeks. She slapped at it, rubbed her face and covered her eyes with her hand. Damn sun. Of all mornings, sleeping in would be heavenly. She was exhausted, darn it, maybe hung-over, and...

Her eyelids shot open.

Where was she?

The...woods. Oh, yeah....

Sitting up, she jerked the cape around her, which was good because she was naked. Her dress was torn to shreds. Crap. And it was on loan. Looking down, she marveled at the slivers of red satin that looked as though they had been ripped with a razor blade.

Or perhaps, claws.

Max? She twisted and glanced about. Her heart sank.

Vanished.

"Oh no..."

What did that mean? Had something gone wrong last night? To her way of thinking everything had gone incredibly, wonderfully, wickedly right. But if that were true, then where was Max?

Where was her mate?

Had he turned wolf? Obviously, she was still human. Were they destined to be star-crossed lovers for the remainder of their days? Overwhelming emotion wracked her and she sank into the cape, her head buried in her hands, tears falling.

A soft pressure landed on her shoulder and slowly, she looked up. Her chest tightened, unsure of what to expect. She glanced up to see who, or what, had touched her.

A breath sucked deep into her throat.

"Max!"

She leaped to her feet and into his arms, the cape and the shards of her dress falling to the ground. He gathered her up and they tumbled back to the ground again, rolling around like kids and puppies.

Except there was nothing kid—or puppy—like about how they were rolling around.

Garnet rained kisses all over his face and then pushed him back and straddled his body, her fists perched on her hips. "Where in the heck were you?" she demanded.

"A bit possessive, my mate?" He tweaked her cheek. "It is quite becoming of you."

She batted his hand away. "Where did you go? I woke up and you were gone. You're not supposed to leave me. I was...."

"Worried?"

"Scared out of my wits."

He fondled one of her breasts. "I needed to stretch my legs. I had quite an evening last night. A bit stiff...."

Garnet paused, and looked down. She reached for the stiff part of him between his legs.

"Ah...stiff?"

He grasped her hands. "Garnet...."

She huffed and feigned anger again, pulling her hands away. "I thought you'd left me, Max LeBlanc. Like, forever! I thought you went all wolf on me or something."

With a twinkle of his golden eyes, he smiled and shook his head. "No, darling. Just part wolf—part man. And that is how I shall remain for all time."

Garnet sat back. "What are you talking about? You're not human? You are still rougarou?"

He nodded. "I'm afraid so. But that is no concern to me now, with you by my side. I wonder, perhaps, if the transition might be more difficult for you, chèr."

She narrowed her gaze and felt the seriousness of his comment. "Um, why for me?" And then she opened her eyes up wide. "Oh, crap. You're kidding. I'm...?"

Max's head dipped in a slow nod. "Yes, *chèr*, you are rougarou now, too. Like your grandmother...and maybe your mother again, too, someday. She is still in mourning. Perhaps that is why she'd never shared your fate with you. And thanks also to some mighty powerful spells cast by your lovely aunt Madeleine."

Garnet clasped a hand over her mouth. "No shit."

Max sat up and wrapped his arms around her waist, then captured her lips in an intoxicating kiss. "No shit," he repeated.

She cocked her head to look at him. "How do you know?"

"Know what? That you are rougarou?"

She nodded. "Yeah, it's not like I have fur or anything, or pointy teeth, or claws, do I?"

Smiling wickedly, he brushed a shock of wayward curls out her eyes, then lowered his hand to run a gentle caress over the small wound on her shoulder where he had marked her.

Lovingly, he stroked her tender skin there.

"Because," he said, his voice a bit raspy, "a rougarou always knows when he's met his mate." He lifted his gaze to peer into her eyes. "I knew from the moment I saw you. It was something about your eyes. And right now, my *chèr*, I have to say you have the most beautiful golden eyes I've ever seen in my life."

She gasped. "My eyes are gold?"

"Honey-gold. Yes. Like mine. Like all rougarous." He peered deep into them. "Are you okay? That your beautiful emerald eyes are now gold?" His voice cracked as he asked the question. She knew the bigger question he was asking. *Are you okay now that you are rougarou?*

Garnet sensed that he was alarmed, and worried that she would not accept her fate. "This will change your life forever."

Garnet didn't think there was any other way she wanted to live. She tilted her head and looked at him. "So, does changing my life forever include experiencing the kind of rip-roaring, howling, wicked lovemaking we had last night? Or was that just a one-time event?"

Max exhaled and a low growl burrowed up from somewhere deep inside him. He nuzzled her neck. "Oh no, *chèr*, not a one-time event. In fact, I plan on a repeat performance very, very soon."

She reached down between them, again grasped his already firm cock, and tenderly stroked it. "Oh my," she whispered, "what a big...."

Max pushed her back to the ground and covered her body with his. "All the better to love you with, *ma chèr*."

MADDIE JAMES

Do you get my Insider News?

Be the first to get the latest news about my books—new releases, free ebooks, sales and discounts, sneak peeks, and exclusive content! Just add your email address at this link:

https://www.maddiejames.net/p/newsletter.html

Bonus! I'll send you a FREE book for signing up.

****

Maddie James writes to silence the people in her head—if only they wouldn't all talk at once!

From flirty contemporary romance to darker erotic titles—often mixed with a dash of suspense or a hint of paranormal—Maddie pens stories that frequently blend a variety of romantic sub-genres. The happily-ever-after, of course, is non-negotiable.

Affaire de Coeur says, "James shows a special talent for traditional romance," and *RT Book Reviews* claims, "James deftly combines romance and suspense." Maddie is the award-winning author of over fifty titles of fiction—from short stories to novels—and a Top 100 Amazon Bestselling Author.

Learn more at http://www.maddiejames.org.

Did you love *Voodoo Bayou*? Then you should read *His Forever Kiss*[1] by Maddie James!

The Forever Trilogy, Book 1 *Can souls touch through time and hold on when all odds are against them?*

Claire Winslow vacations on an East Coast barrier island, content with her life and her potential future—until the illusion of a man walking the misty shore haunts her. Then one kiss—a beautiful, soulful, stolen kiss in the night—and her life changes forever.

Nearly 300 years past, Jack Porter is in hot pursuit of his kidnapped wife. Not an easy feat considering the year is 1718 and the kidnapper is the notorious pirate Blackbeard aka Edward Teach. Determined to rescue his wife and take the pirate's head in the process, Jack steals aboard the pirate's ship to save her.

---

1. https://books2read.com/u/bpG91W

2. https://books2read.com/u/bpG91W

His Forever Kiss sends Jack and Claire on a wild search through time, not only for the resolution to a powerful attraction between them, but also for a historical artifact that holds the key to their future happiness—the coveted silver-plated chalice made from Blackbeard's skull.

Read more at www.maddiejames.org.

Also by Maddie James

A Dickens Holiday Romance
Christmas in July

A Harbor Falls Romance
All of My Heart
Dance into My Heart
Perfectly Matched
Sweet Hart Inn at Harbor Falls: A Small Town, Second Chance
Romance

Colorado Dreamin'
Rawhide & Roses
Broken
The Cowboy's Secret Baby

Ghosts of Carrington
Freshly Dead
Seriously Dead

Gratefully Dead
Digging the Dead Guys

Rock Creek Ranch
Callie's Wedding

The Charmington Series
Home for Christmas
Miracle at Holly Hill Inn
The Last Christmas at Holly Hill Inn
Charming the Prince
Christmas at Holly Hill Inn

The Forever Trilogy
The Forever Trilogy
His Forever Kiss
Her Forever Love
Her Forever Dream

The Parker Ranches
Parker: Rock Creek Ranch
Corporate Cowboy
Protecting Sarah
Jake's Temptation
Ethan: Black Sheep Cowboy
Leaving Noah

Evan: Kiss Me Again, Cowboy
A Cowboy Christmas at Rock Creek Ranch
Callie

The Parker Ranches, Inc.
The Rancher's Second Chance: Rock Creek Ranch
Rock Creek Ranch Box Set

Standalone
Tempt Me
Safe Haven
The Last Blue-Eyed Woman
A Perfect Escape
Double Crossed
Protect Me Not
Voodoo Bayou
Don't Tempt Me
What Doesn't Kill You
Colorado Dreamin' Duet
Discover Your Write Path to Publishing Success
Cowboys and Ranchers
Ways to Wreck a Wedding (and still get a happy ending)

Watch for more at www.maddiejames.org.

About the Author

Writing flirty contemporary romance, mystery and suspense, and upmarket women's fiction.

Maddie James writes stories from the heartland, from small towns to ranches. As M.L. Jameson, she pens gritty paranormal and romantic suspense. Madeleine Jaimes writes upmarket women's fiction focused on friendships and relationships.

In 2022, Maddie celebrated her 25th year of publishing romance fiction, with nearly 80 published titles to date. Affair de Coeur claimed Maddie, "shows a special talent for traditional romance," and RT Book Reviews said, "James deftly combines romance and suspense, so hope on for an exhilarating ride."

Read more at www.maddiejames.org.